W9-BCO-954

THE BRAIN
A GRAPHIC NOVEL TOUR

written by
Joeming Dunn
illustrated by
Rod Espinosa

visit us at
www.abdopublishing.com

Published by Magic Wagon, a division of the ABDO Group, 8000 West 78ᵗʰ Street, Edina, Minnesota 55439. Copyright © 2010 by Abdo Consulting Group, Inc. International copyrights reserved in all countries. All rights reserved. No part of this book may be reproduced in any form without written permission from the publisher.

Graphic Planet™ is a trademark and logo of Magic Wagon.

Printed in the United States.

 Manufactured with paper containing at least 10% post-consumer waste

Text by Joeming Dunn
Illustrated by Rod Espinosa
Colored and lettered by Rod Espinosa
Edited by Stephanie Hedlund
Interior layout and design by Antarctic Press
Cover art by Rod Espinosa
Cover design by Neil Klinepier

Library of Congress Cataloging-in-Publication Data

Dunn, Joeming W.
 The brain : a graphic novel tour / by Joeming Dunn ; illustrated by Rod Espinosa.
 p. cm. -- (Graphic adventures. The human body)
 Includes index
 ISBN 978-1-60270-683-5

 1. Brain--Juvenile literature 2. Graphic novels--Juvenile literature. I. Espinosa, Rod. Ill. II. Title.

QP376.D86 2010
612.8'2--dc22

                                                2009017650

TABLE of CONTENTS

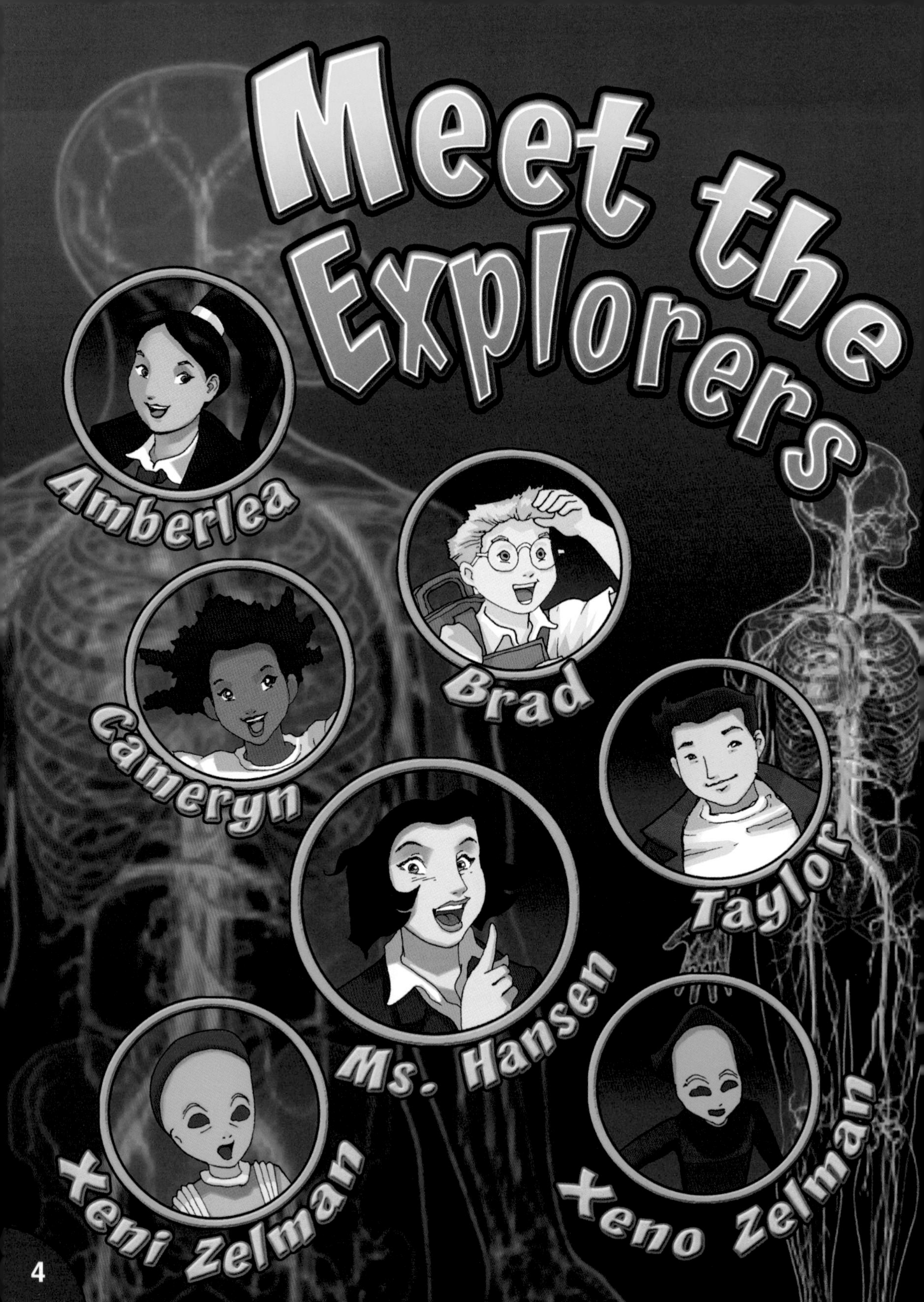
Meet the Explorers
Amberlea
Brad
Cameryn
Taylor
Ms. Hansen
Xeni Zelman
Xeno Zelman

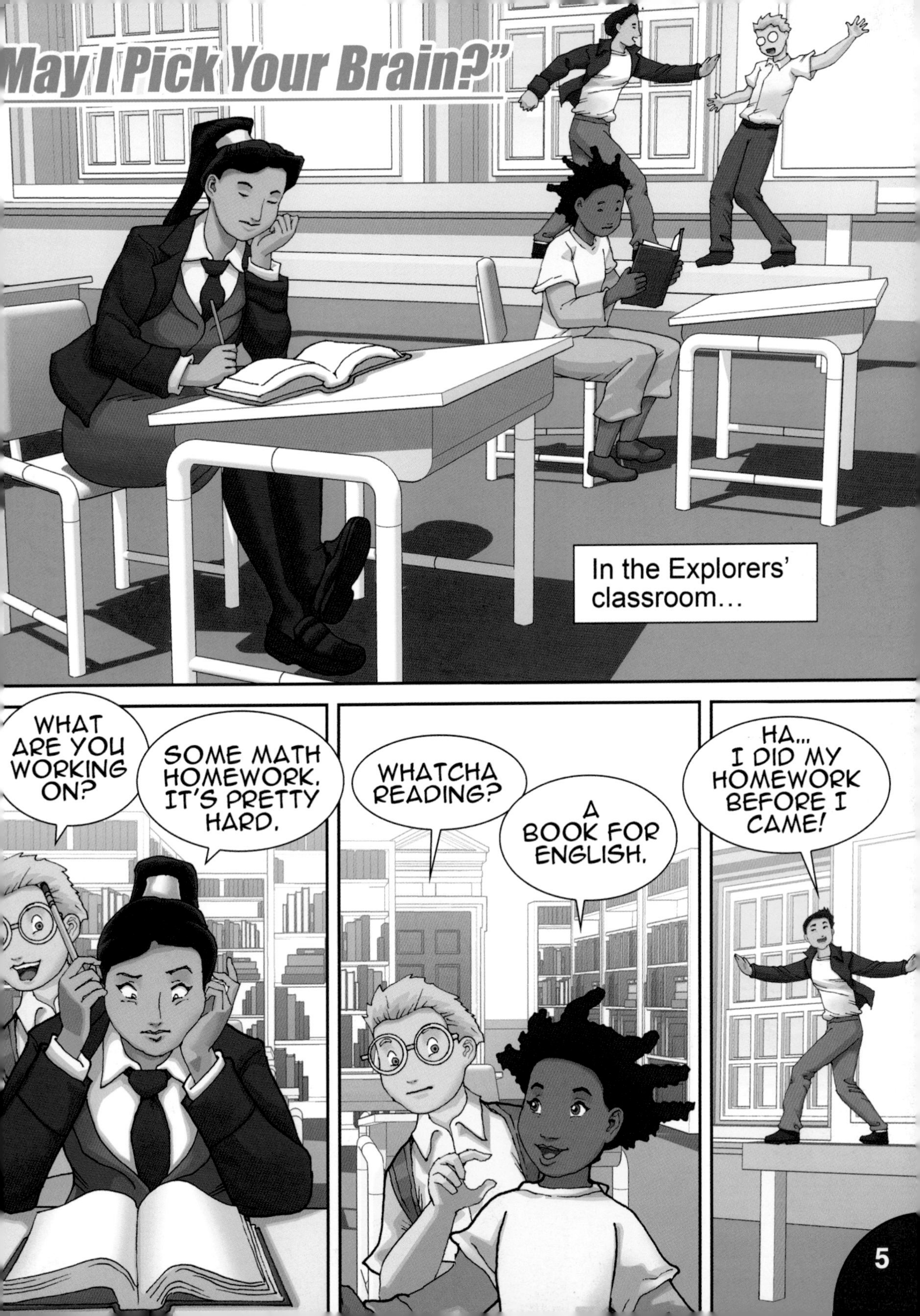
May I Pick Your Brain?”
In the Explorers’ classroom…
WHAT ARE YOU WORKING ON?
SOME MATH HOMEWORK. IT’S PRETTY HARD.
WHATCHA READING?
A BOOK FOR ENGLISH.
HA... I DID MY HOMEWORK BEFORE I CAME!

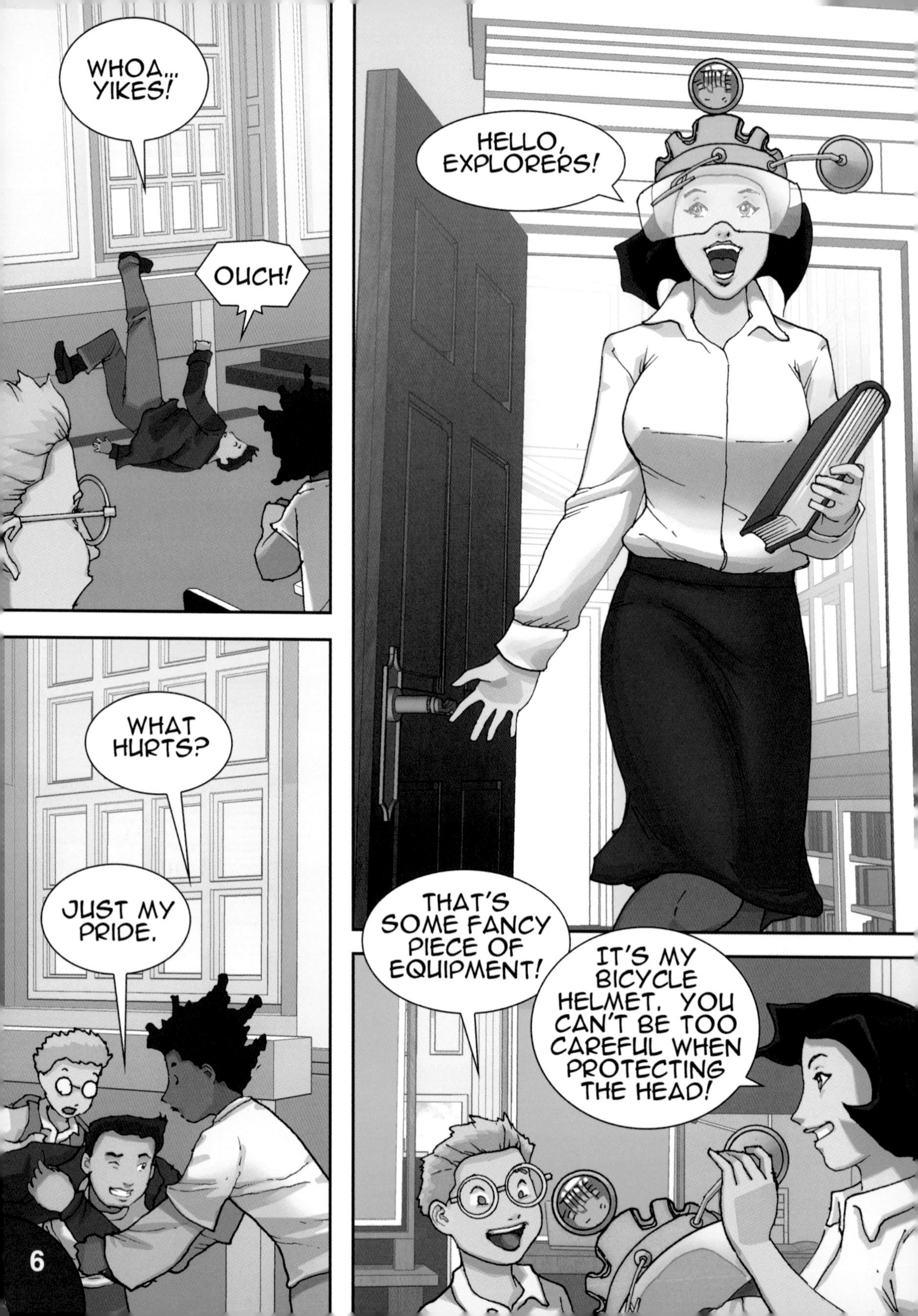
WHOA... YIKES!
OUCH!
WHAT HURTS?
JUST MY PRIDE.
HELLO, EXPLORERS!
THAT'S SOME FANCY PIECE OF EQUIPMENT!
IT'S MY BICYCLE HELMET. YOU CAN'T BE TOO CAREFUL WHEN PROTECTING THE HEAD!

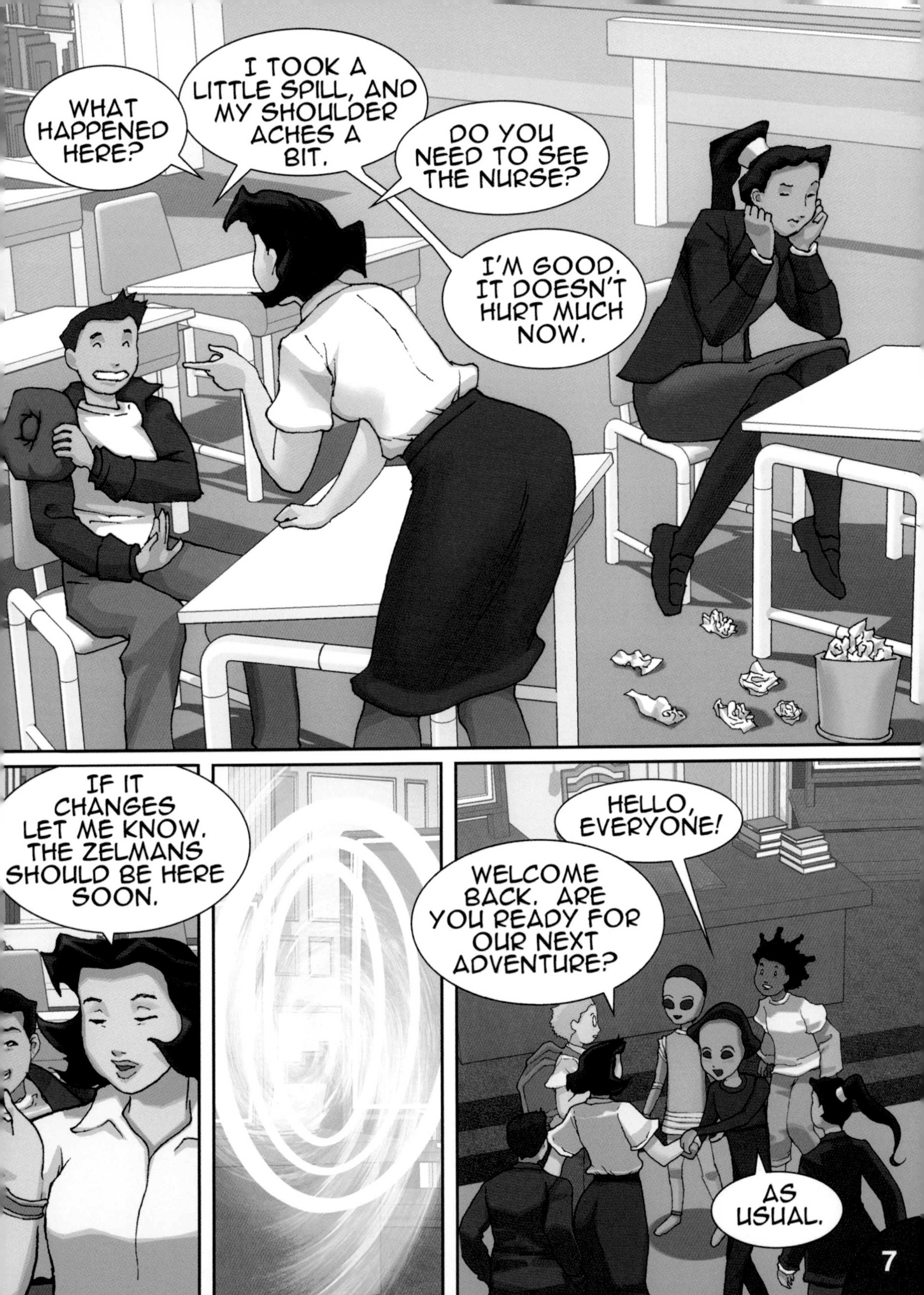
WHAT HAPPENED HERE?
I TOOK A LITTLE SPILL, AND MY SHOULDER ACHES A BIT.
DO YOU NEED TO SEE THE NURSE?
I'M GOOD. IT DOESN'T HURT MUCH NOW.
IF IT CHANGES LET ME KNOW. THE ZELMANS SHOULD BE HERE SOON.
HELLO, EVERYONE!
WELCOME BACK. ARE YOU READY FOR OUR NEXT ADVENTURE?
AS USUAL.

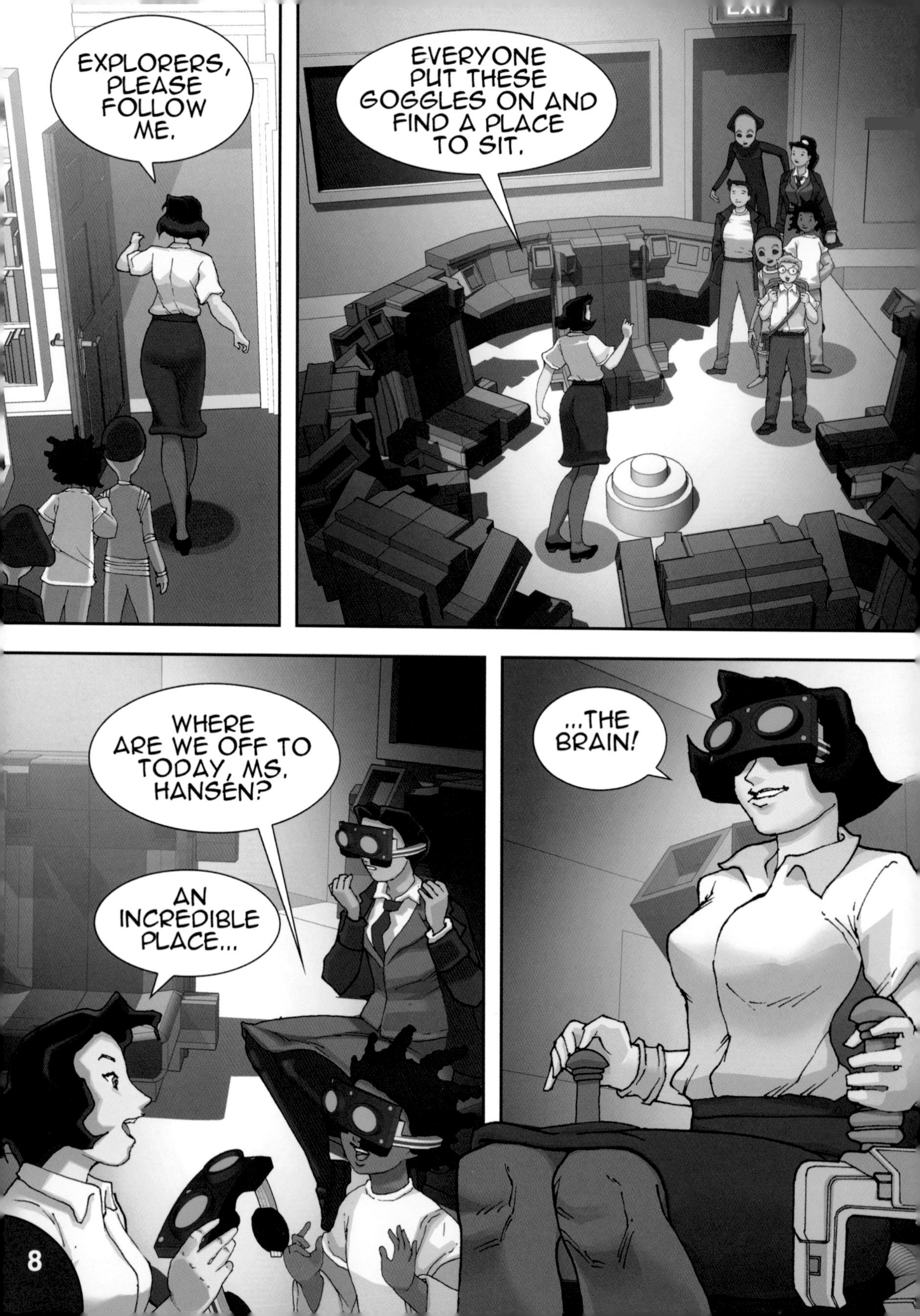
EXPLORERS, PLEASE FOLLOW ME.
EVERYONE PUT THESE GOGGLES ON AND FIND A PLACE TO SIT.
WHERE ARE WE OFF TO TODAY, MS. HANSEN?
AN INCREDIBLE PLACE...
...THE BRAIN!

THE BRAIN IS PART OF THE NERVOUS SYSTEM.

THE NERVOUS SYSTEM IS HOW THE BODY COMMUNICATES WITH ITSELF.

THE BRAIN IS THE CENTRAL COMPUTER OR CONDUCTOR TO THE ENTIRE SYSTEM. TOGETHER, THE BRAIN AND THE SPINAL CORD ARE CALLED THE CENTRAL NERVOUS SYSTEM.

EWW...THE BRAIN LOOKS LIKE A BIG BLOB!

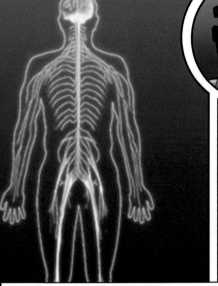

ALL THE NERVES, OR "WIRES," GO OUT TO THE REST OF THE BODY. THIS IS CALLED THE PERIPHERAL NERVOUS SYSTEM.

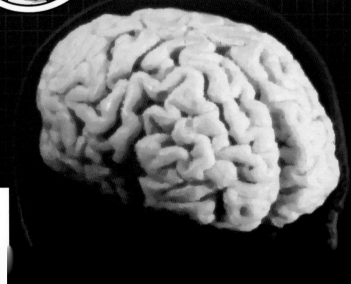

JUST THINK OF IT AS TELEPHONE WIRES GOING THROUGHOUT THE BODY.

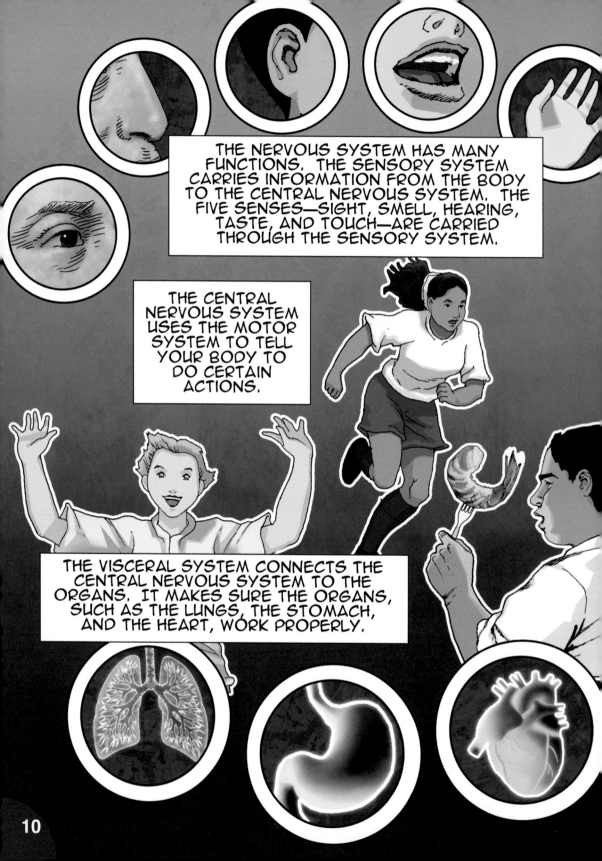

THE NERVOUS SYSTEM HAS MANY FUNCTIONS. THE SENSORY SYSTEM CARRIES INFORMATION FROM THE BODY TO THE CENTRAL NERVOUS SYSTEM. THE FIVE SENSES—SIGHT, SMELL, HEARING, TASTE, AND TOUCH—ARE CARRIED THROUGH THE SENSORY SYSTEM.

THE CENTRAL NERVOUS SYSTEM USES THE MOTOR SYSTEM TO TELL YOUR BODY TO DO CERTAIN ACTIONS.

THE VISCERAL SYSTEM CONNECTS THE CENTRAL NERVOUS SYSTEM TO THE ORGANS. IT MAKES SURE THE ORGANS, SUCH AS THE LUNGS, THE STOMACH, AND THE HEART, WORK PROPERLY.

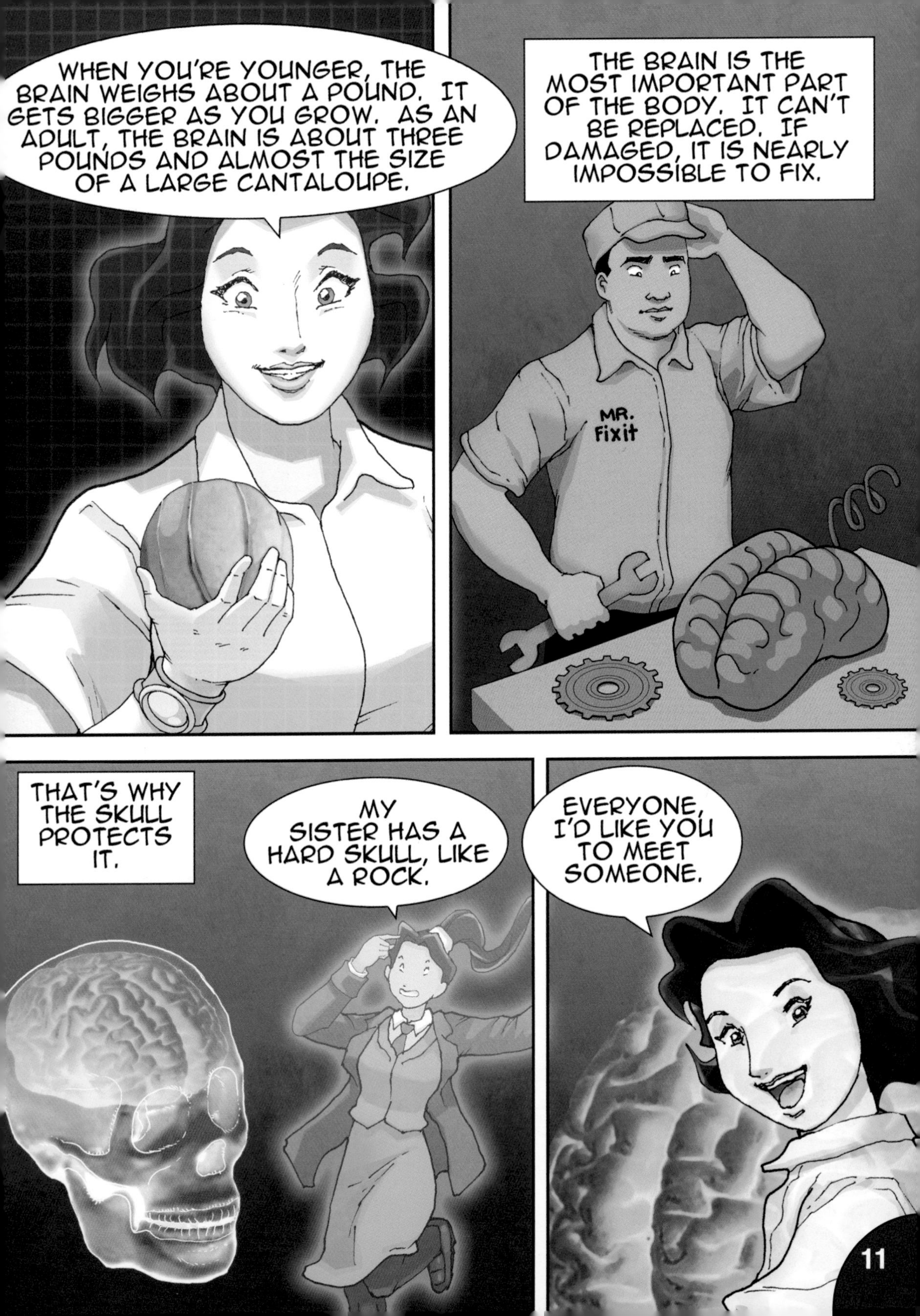
WHEN YOU'RE YOUNGER, THE BRAIN WEIGHS ABOUT A POUND. IT GETS BIGGER AS YOU GROW. AS AN ADULT, THE BRAIN IS ABOUT THREE POUNDS AND ALMOST THE SIZE OF A LARGE CANTALOUPE.
THE BRAIN IS THE MOST IMPORTANT PART OF THE BODY. IT CAN'T BE REPLACED. IF DAMAGED, IT IS NEARLY IMPOSSIBLE TO FIX.
MR. Fixit
THAT'S WHY THE SKULL PROTECTS IT.
MY SISTER HAS A HARD SKULL, LIKE A ROCK.
EVERYONE, I'D LIKE YOU TO MEET SOMEONE.

CLASS, THIS IS DR. NEURON.

HELLO!

HOWDY!

I'M GLAD YOU COULD COME AND VISIT. MY FRIENDS AND I MAKE UP THE BULK OF THE NERVOUS SYSTEM.

A NEURON IS MADE OF THREE MAIN COMPONENTS. THE FIRST IS THE CELL BODY, WHICH CONTAINS MOST OF THE INFORMATION OF THE CELL. THE SECOND IS THE AXON, WHICH CARRIES SIGNALS AWAY FROM THE NEURON. SOME AXONS ARE VERY SHORT, BUT SOME STRETCH FROM YOUR BRAIN TO YOUR TOES!

THE LAST COMPONENT OF THE NEURON IS THE DENDRITES. THEY ARE HOW THE NEURONS COMMUNICATE WITH EACH OTHER AND WITH OTHER PARTS OF THE BODY. THEY DO THIS BY SENDING OUT CHEMICALS BETWEEN SPECIAL CONNECTIONS CALLED SYNAPSES.

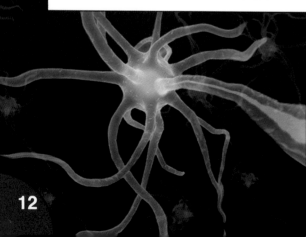

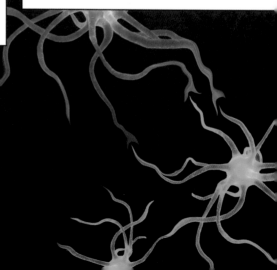

IN THE BRAIN ITSELF, THERE ARE QUITE OF FEW OF US AROUND!

THE BRAIN IS MADE UP OF MORE THAN 100 BILLION NEURONS.

100,000,000,000

THE NEURONS BUNCH TOGETHER TO FORM THE NERVES THAT RUN THROUGHOUT THE BODY. THEY WORK TOGETHER.

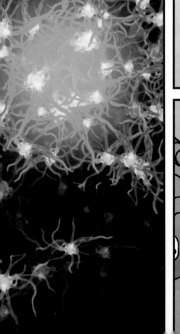

WHENEVER THE BRAIN TELLS US SOMETHING, WE HAVE TO ACT FAST. THE HARDER THE TASK, THE MORE NEURONS IN THE NERVE WILL SEND THE SIGNAL.

TELL THE HAND TO DO THIS!

RIGHT AWAY!

SOME TRANSMISSIONS TRAVEL AT 250 MILES PER HOUR!

Whoosh!

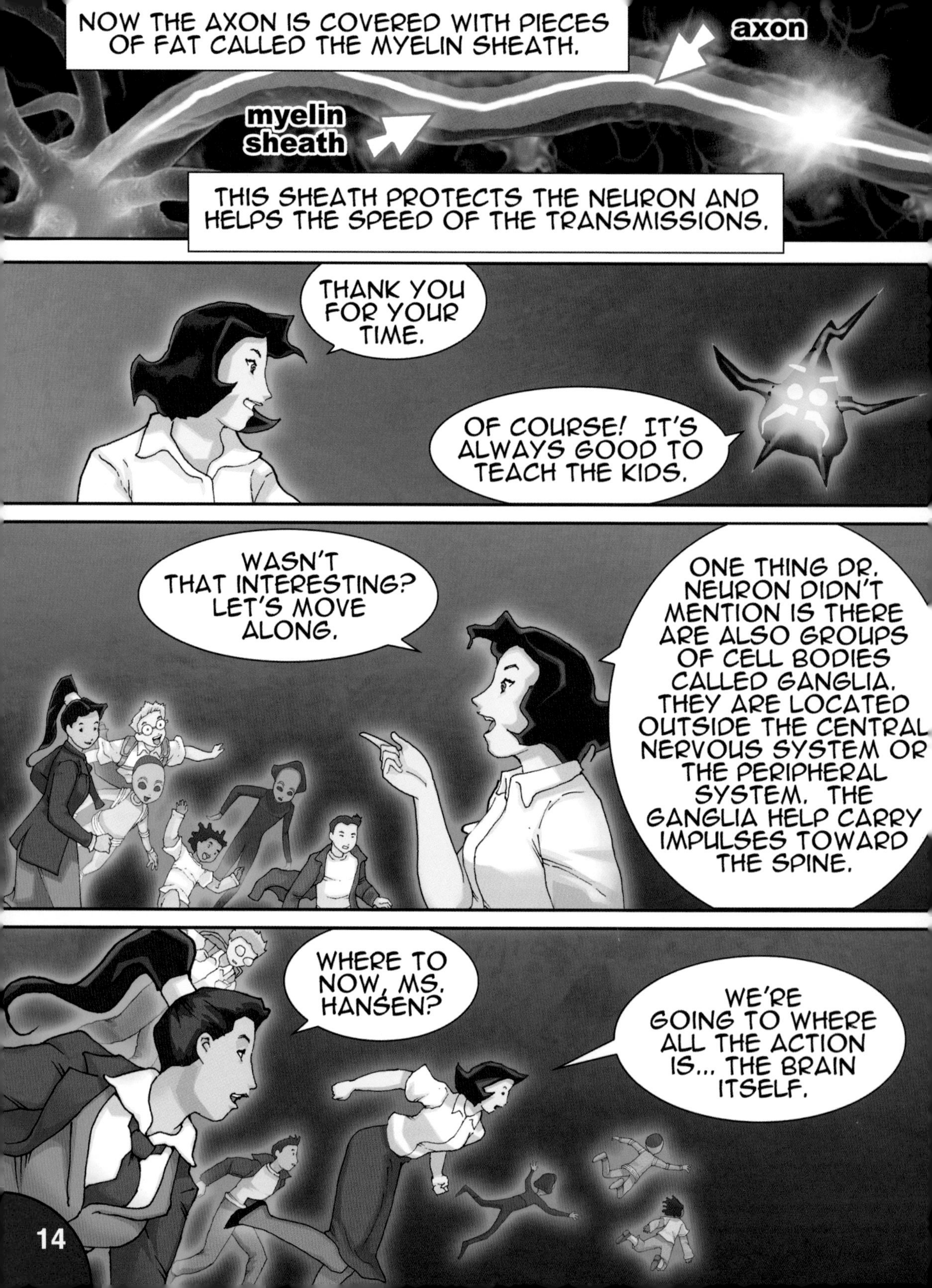
NOW THE AXON IS COVERED WITH PIECES OF FAT CALLED THE MYELIN SHEATH.
axon
myelin sheath
THIS SHEATH PROTECTS THE NEURON AND HELPS THE SPEED OF THE TRANSMISSIONS.
THANK YOU FOR YOUR TIME.
OF COURSE! IT'S ALWAYS GOOD TO TEACH THE KIDS.
WASN'T THAT INTERESTING? LET'S MOVE ALONG.
ONE THING DR. NEURON DIDN'T MENTION IS THERE ARE ALSO GROUPS OF CELL BODIES CALLED GANGLIA. THEY ARE LOCATED OUTSIDE THE CENTRAL NERVOUS SYSTEM OR THE PERIPHERAL SYSTEM. THE GANGLIA HELP CARRY IMPULSES TOWARD THE SPINE.
WHERE TO NOW, MS. HANSEN?
WE'RE GOING TO WHERE ALL THE ACTION IS... THE BRAIN ITSELF.

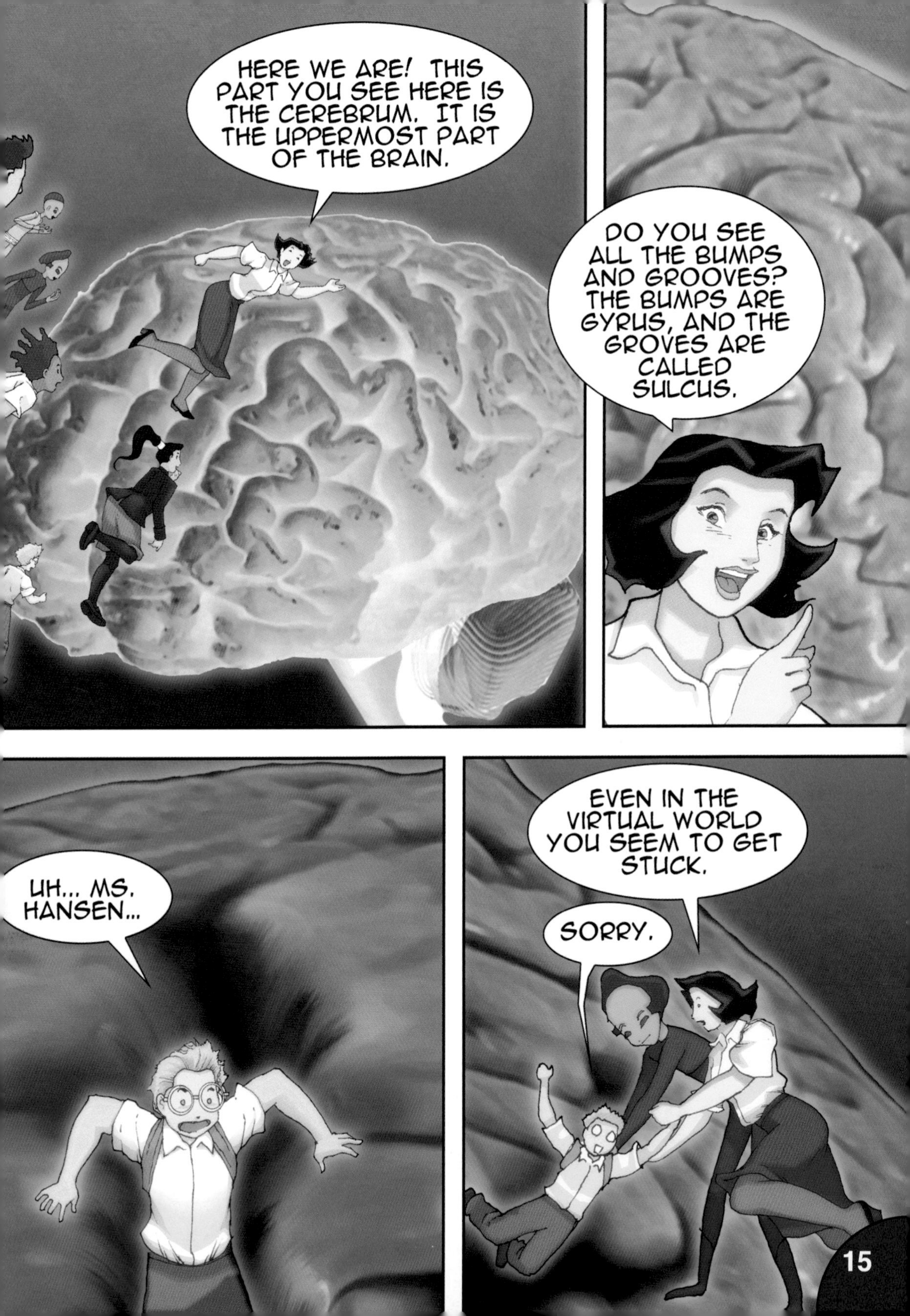
HERE WE ARE! THIS PART YOU SEE HERE IS THE CEREBRUM. IT IS THE UPPERMOST PART OF THE BRAIN.
DO YOU SEE ALL THE BUMPS AND GROOVES? THE BUMPS ARE GYRUS, AND THE GROVES ARE CALLED SULCUS.
UH... MS. HANSEN...
EVEN IN THE VIRTUAL WORLD YOU SEEM TO GET STUCK.
SORRY.

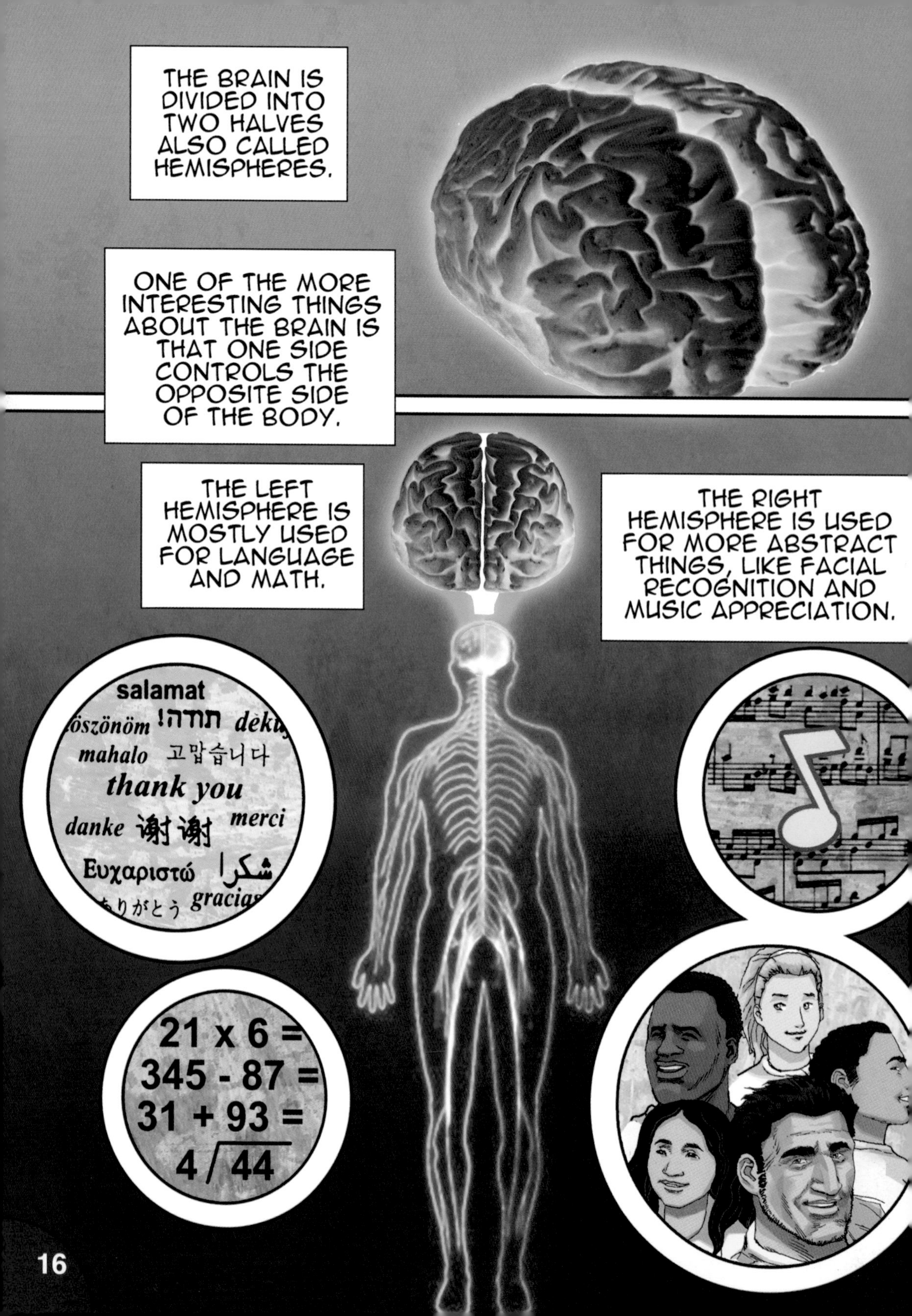

THE BRAIN IS DIVIDED INTO TWO HALVES ALSO CALLED HEMISPHERES.

ONE OF THE MORE INTERESTING THINGS ABOUT THE BRAIN IS THAT ONE SIDE CONTROLS THE OPPOSITE SIDE OF THE BODY.

THE LEFT HEMISPHERE IS MOSTLY USED FOR LANGUAGE AND MATH.

THE RIGHT HEMISPHERE IS USED FOR MORE ABSTRACT THINGS, LIKE FACIAL RECOGNITION AND MUSIC APPRECIATION.

salamat
köszönöm! תודה dekuji
mahalo 고맙습니다
thank you
danke 谢谢 merci
Ευχαριστώ شكرا
ありがとう gracias

21 x 6 =
345 - 87 =
31 + 93 =
4 / 44

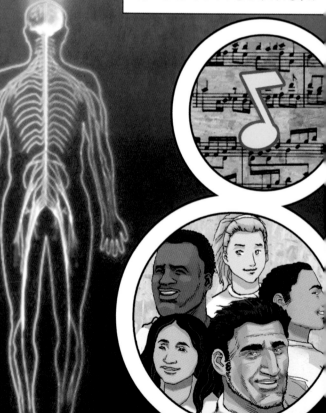

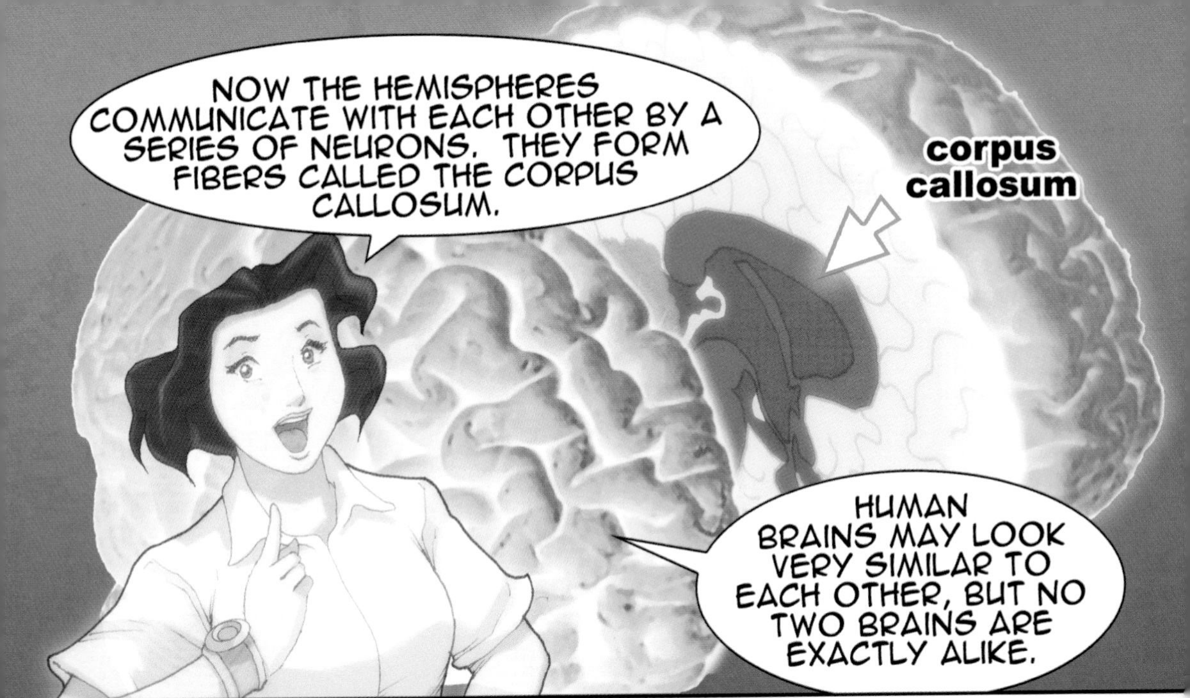
NOW THE HEMISPHERES COMMUNICATE WITH EACH OTHER BY A SERIES OF NEURONS. THEY FORM FIBERS CALLED THE CORPUS CALLOSUM.
corpus callosum
HUMAN BRAINS MAY LOOK VERY SIMILAR TO EACH OTHER, BUT NO TWO BRAINS ARE EXACTLY ALIKE.

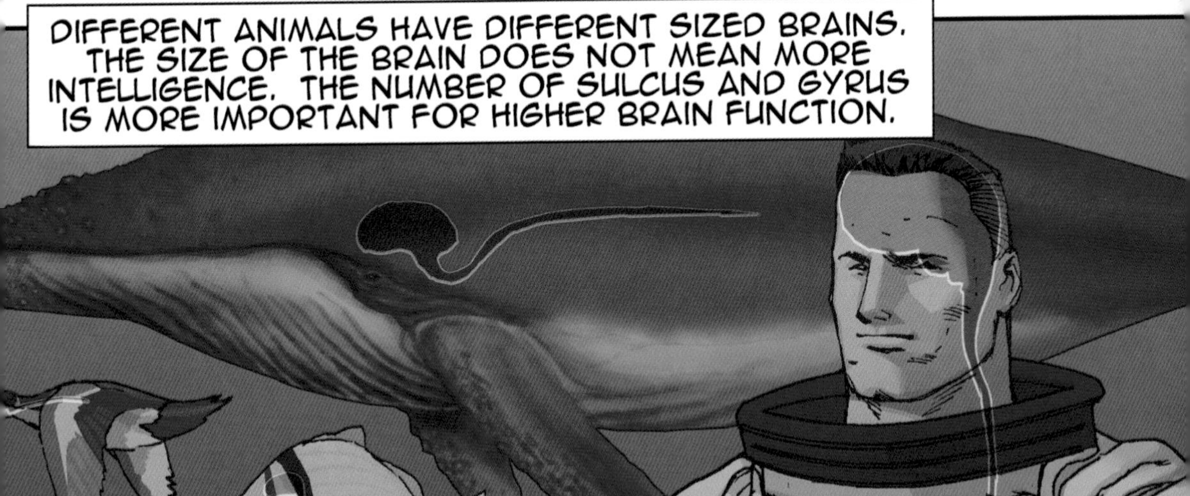
DIFFERENT ANIMALS HAVE DIFFERENT SIZED BRAINS. THE SIZE OF THE BRAIN DOES NOT MEAN MORE INTELLIGENCE. THE NUMBER OF SULCUS AND GYRUS IS MORE IMPORTANT FOR HIGHER BRAIN FUNCTION.

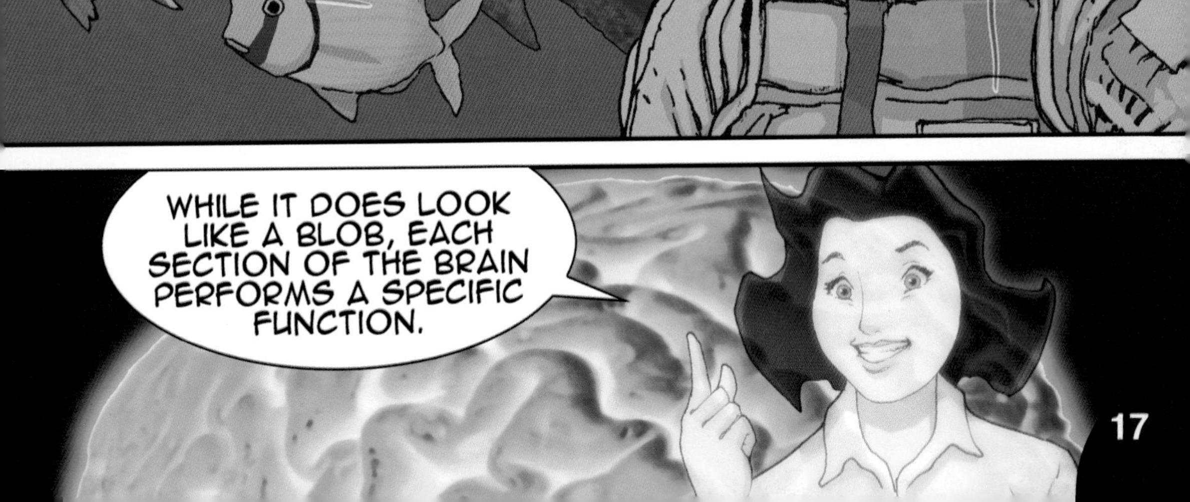
WHILE IT DOES LOOK LIKE A BLOB, EACH SECTION OF THE BRAIN PERFORMS A SPECIFIC FUNCTION.

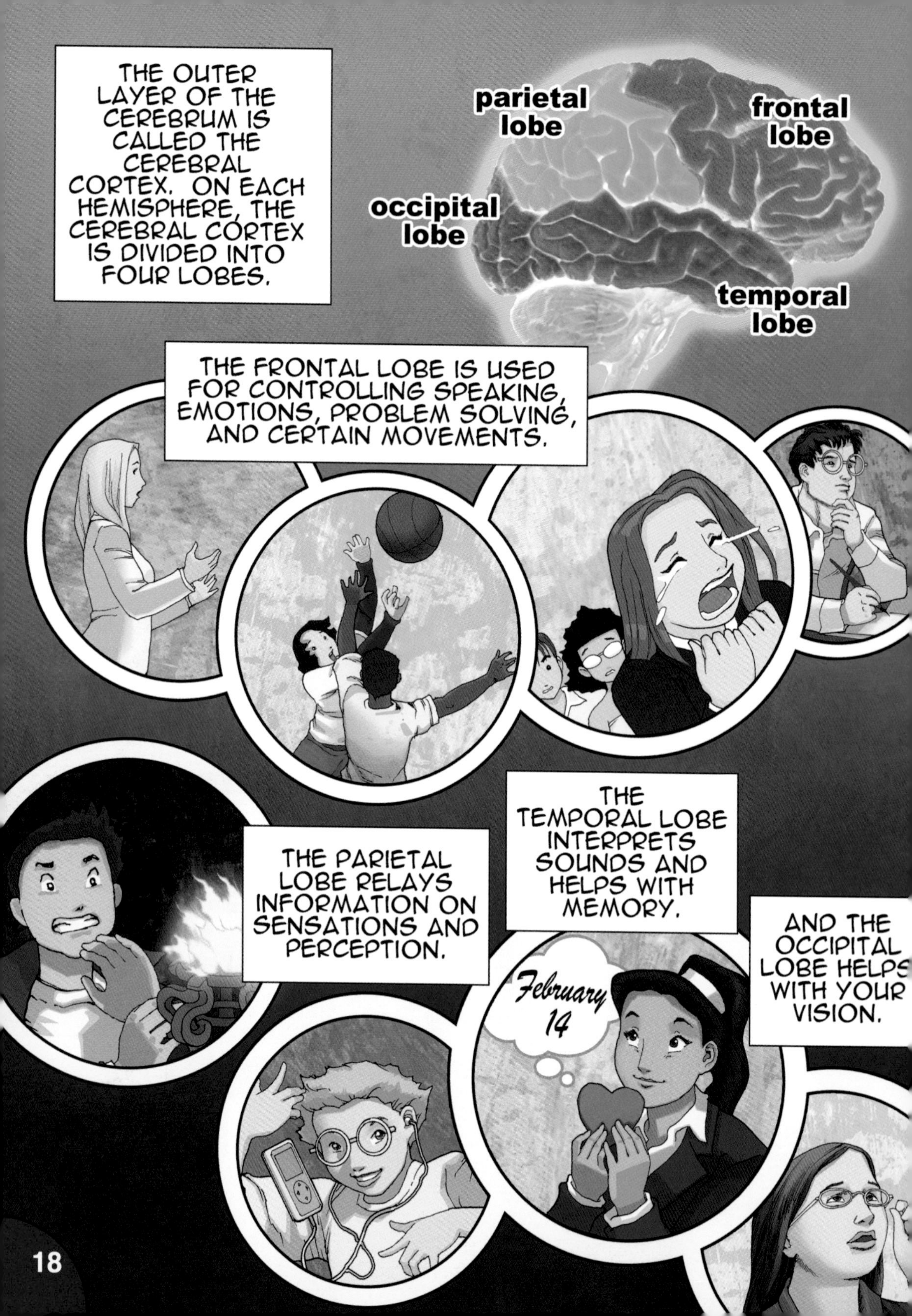
THE OUTER LAYER OF THE CEREBRUM IS CALLED THE CEREBRAL CORTEX. ON EACH HEMISPHERE, THE CEREBRAL CORTEX IS DIVIDED INTO FOUR LOBES.
parietal lobe
frontal lobe
occipital lobe
temporal lobe
THE FRONTAL LOBE IS USED FOR CONTROLLING SPEAKING, EMOTIONS, PROBLEM SOLVING, AND CERTAIN MOVEMENTS.
THE PARIETAL LOBE RELAYS INFORMATION ON SENSATIONS AND PERCEPTION.
THE TEMPORAL LOBE INTERPRETS SOUNDS AND HELPS WITH MEMORY.
February 14
AND THE OCCIPITAL LOBE HELPS WITH YOUR VISION.

MS. HANSEN, WHAT PART OF THE BRAIN IS THIS? IT DOESN'T LOOK LIKE THE FRONT PART.
THAT, TAYLOR, IS THE CEREBELLUM, WHICH IS ALSO CALLED THE LITTLE BRAIN.
THE CEREBELLUM'S MAIN FUNCTION IS TO COORDINATE MOVEMENT, SUCH AS BALANCE OR POSTURE.
BRAD COULD USE AN EXTRA HELPING OF THAT PART OF THE BRAIN!

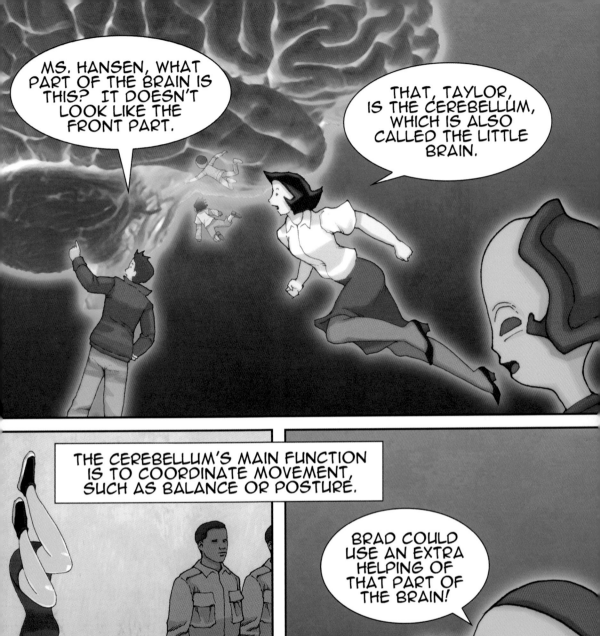

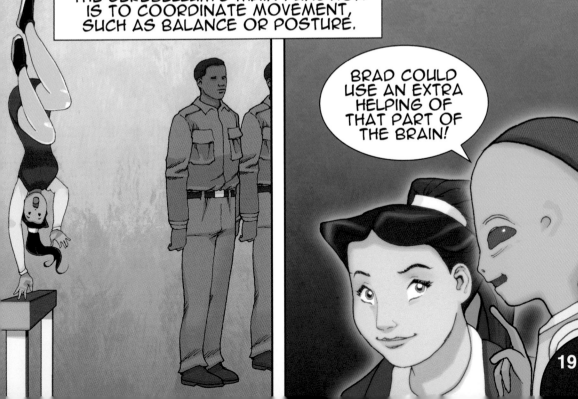

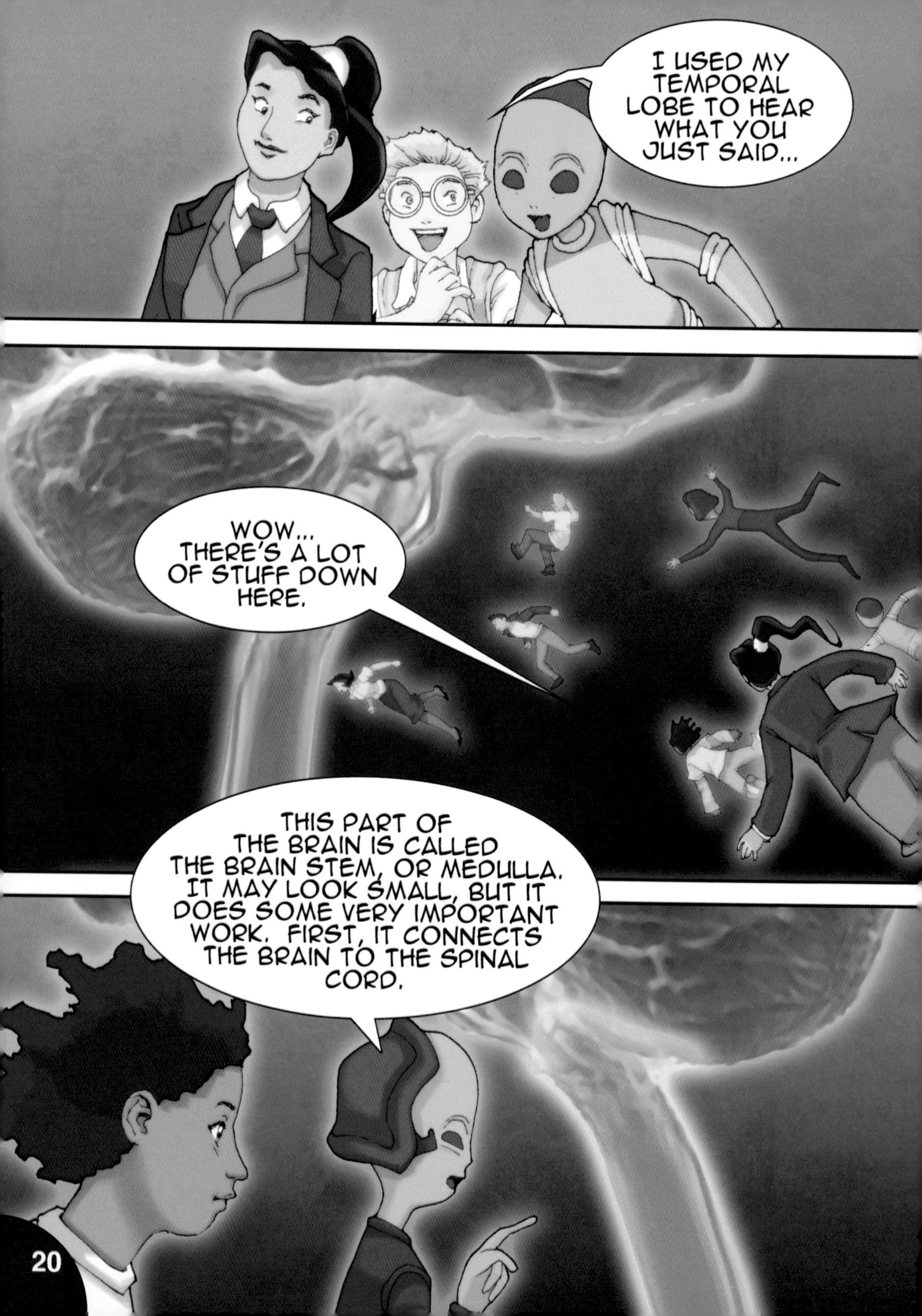
I USED MY TEMPORAL LOBE TO HEAR WHAT YOU JUST SAID...
WOW... THERE'S A LOT OF STUFF DOWN HERE.
THIS PART OF THE BRAIN IS CALLED THE BRAIN STEM, OR MEDULLA. IT MAY LOOK SMALL, BUT IT DOES SOME VERY IMPORTANT WORK. FIRST, IT CONNECTS THE BRAIN TO THE SPINAL CORD.

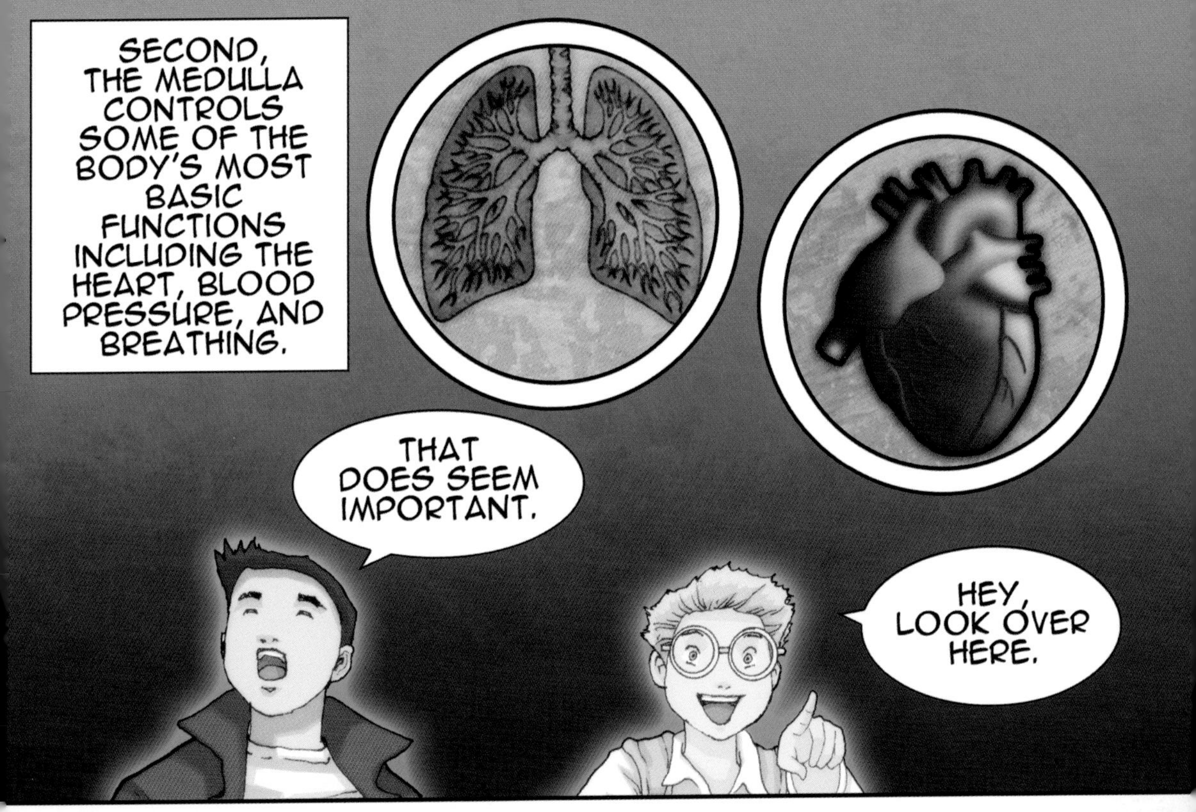
SECOND, THE MEDULLA CONTROLS SOME OF THE BODY'S MOST BASIC FUNCTIONS INCLUDING THE HEART, BLOOD PRESSURE, AND BREATHING.
THAT DOES SEEM IMPORTANT.
HEY, LOOK OVER HERE.

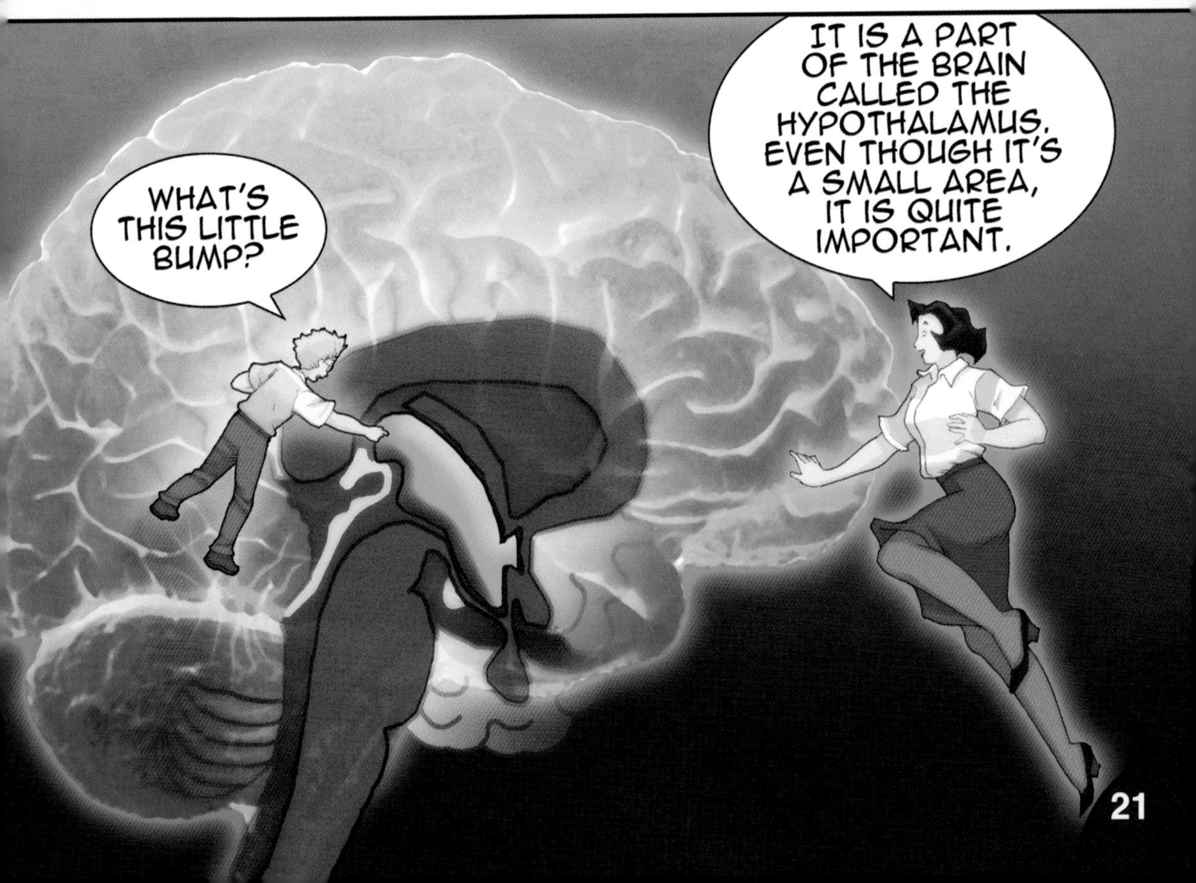
WHAT'S THIS LITTLE BUMP?
IT IS A PART OF THE BRAIN CALLED THE HYPOTHALAMUS. EVEN THOUGH IT'S A SMALL AREA, IT IS QUITE IMPORTANT.

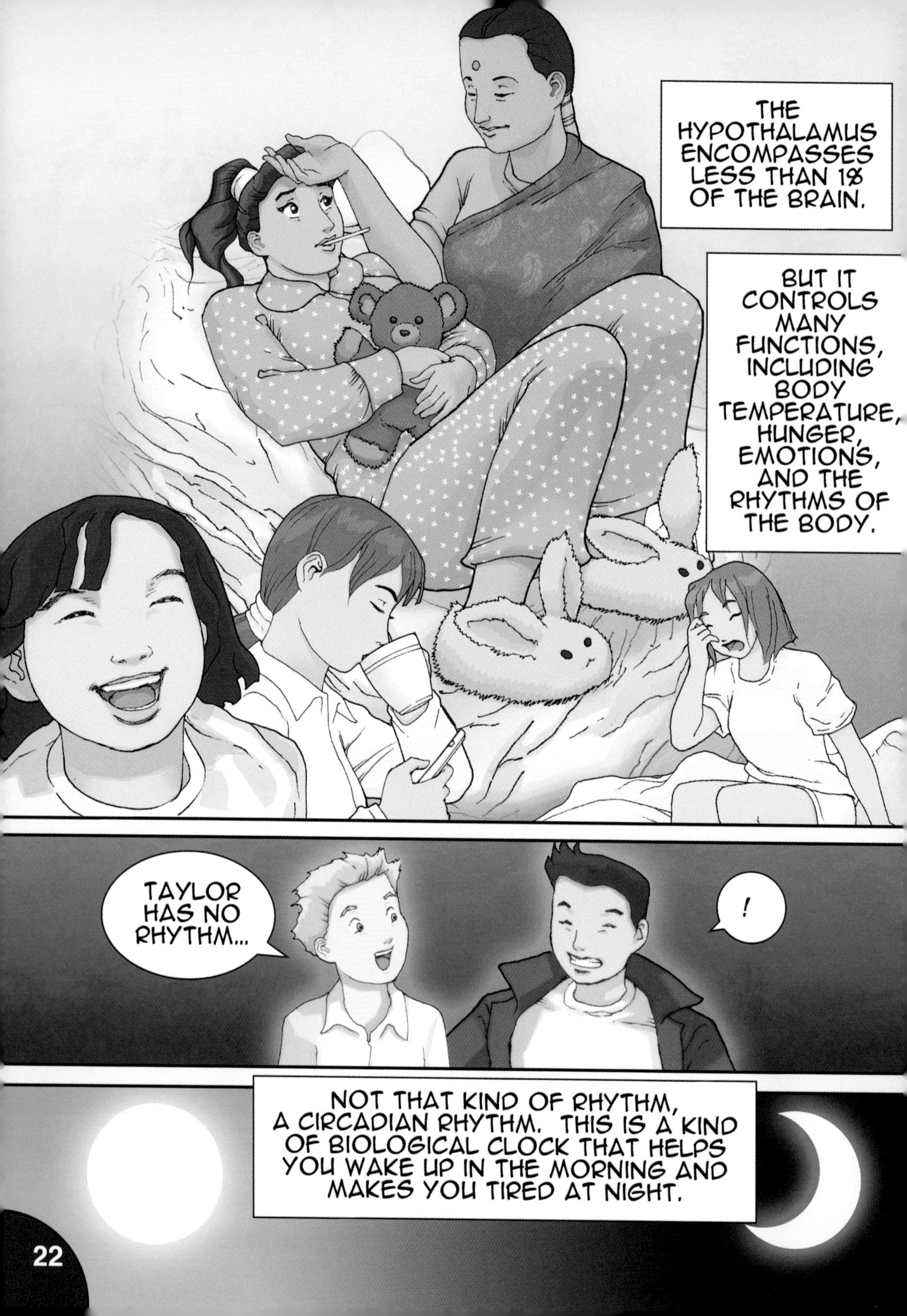
THE HYPOTHALAMUS ENCOMPASSES LESS THAN 1% OF THE BRAIN.
BUT IT CONTROLS MANY FUNCTIONS, INCLUDING BODY TEMPERATURE, HUNGER, EMOTIONS, AND THE RHYTHMS OF THE BODY.
TAYLOR HAS NO RHYTHM...
!
NOT THAT KIND OF RHYTHM, A CIRCADIAN RHYTHM. THIS IS A KIND OF BIOLOGICAL CLOCK THAT HELPS YOU WAKE UP IN THE MORNING AND MAKES YOU TIRED AT NIGHT.

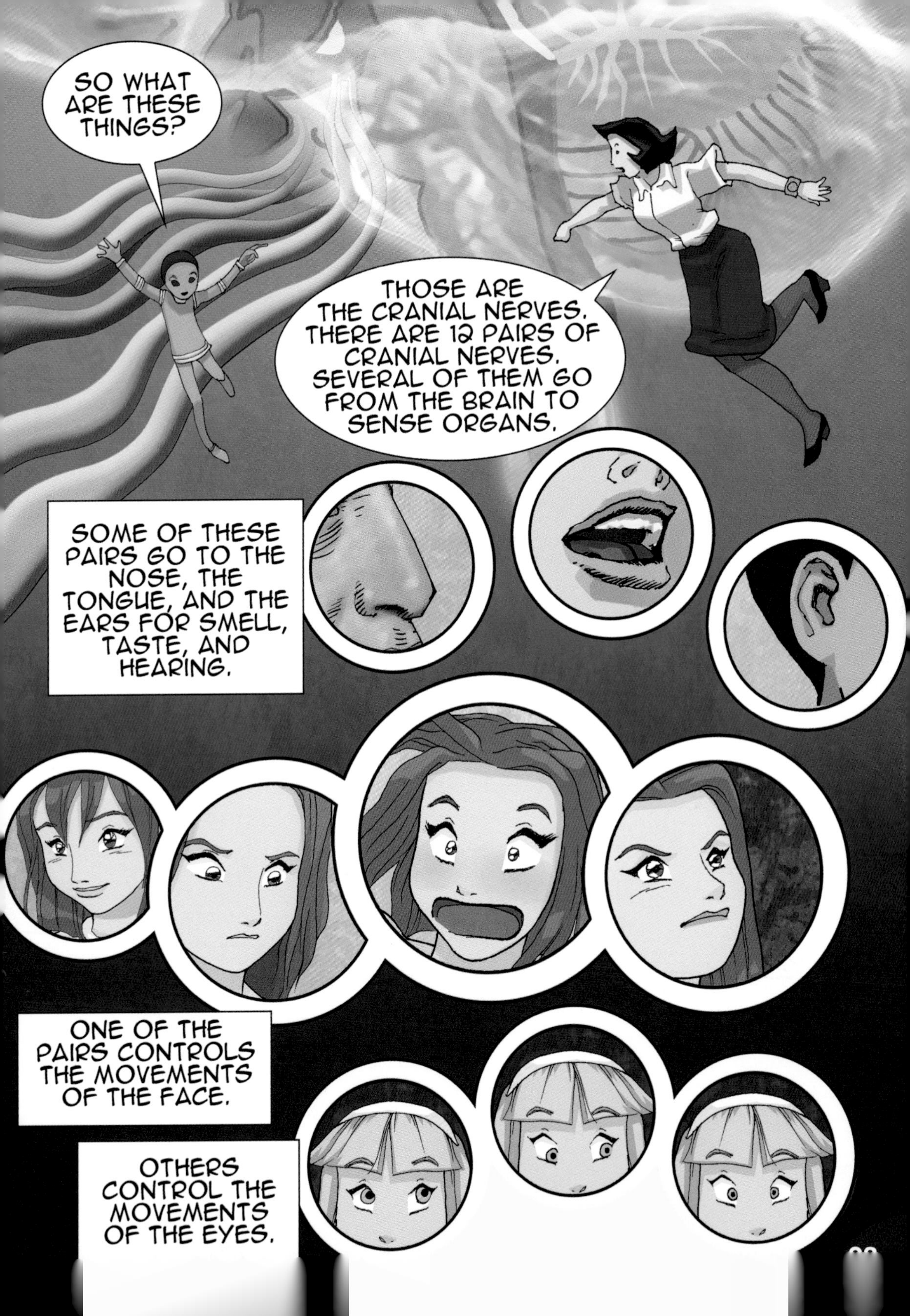
SO WHAT ARE THESE THINGS?
THOSE ARE THE CRANIAL NERVES. THERE ARE 12 PAIRS OF CRANIAL NERVES. SEVERAL OF THEM GO FROM THE BRAIN TO SENSE ORGANS.
SOME OF THESE PAIRS GO TO THE NOSE, THE TONGUE, AND THE EARS FOR SMELL, TASTE, AND HEARING.
ONE OF THE PAIRS CONTROLS THE MOVEMENTS OF THE FACE.
OTHERS CONTROL THE MOVEMENTS OF THE EYES.

THERE ARE TWO MAJOR THINGS, BESIDES THE SKULL, THAT PROTECT THE BRAIN.

THE FIRST IS A MEMBRANE THAT ACTS LIKE A CASTLE WALL. THIS SPECIAL BARRIER IS BETWEEN THE SKULL AND THE BRAIN. IT'S MADE OF THREE MEMBRANES CALLED MENINGES.

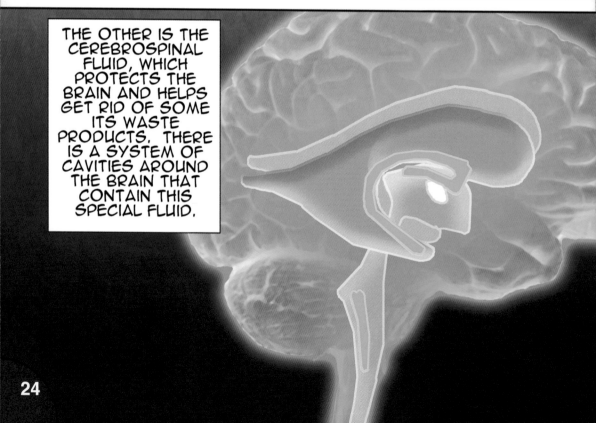

THE OTHER IS THE CEREBROSPINAL FLUID, WHICH PROTECTS THE BRAIN AND HELPS GET RID OF SOME ITS WASTE PRODUCTS. THERE IS A SYSTEM OF CAVITIES AROUND THE BRAIN THAT CONTAIN THIS SPECIAL FLUID.

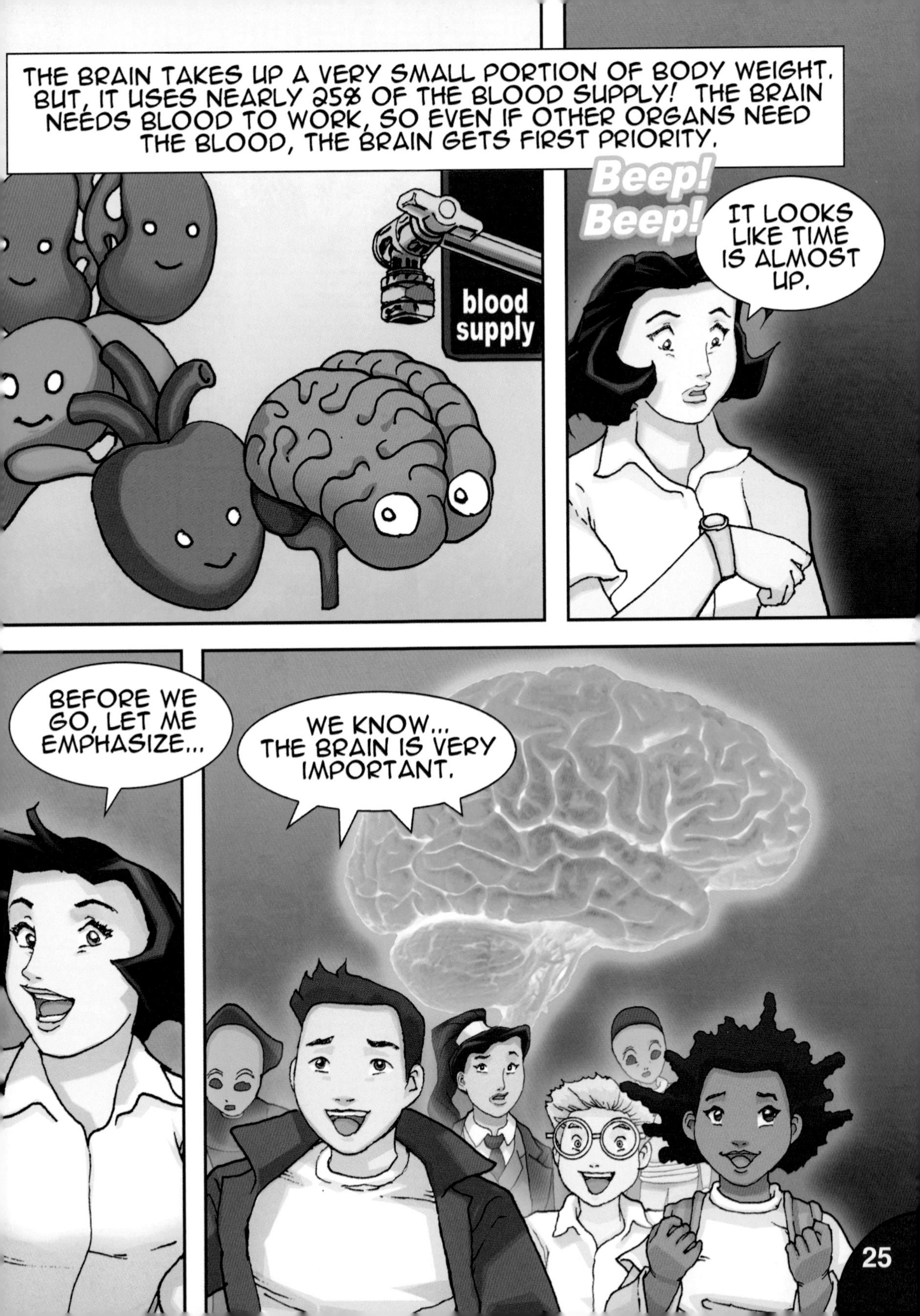
THE BRAIN TAKES UP A VERY SMALL PORTION OF BODY WEIGHT. BUT, IT USES NEARLY 25% OF THE BLOOD SUPPLY! THE BRAIN NEEDS BLOOD TO WORK, SO EVEN IF OTHER ORGANS NEED THE BLOOD, THE BRAIN GETS FIRST PRIORITY.
blood supply
Beep! Beep!
IT LOOKS LIKE TIME IS ALMOST UP.
BEFORE WE GO, LET ME EMPHASIZE...
WE KNOW... THE BRAIN IS VERY IMPORTANT.

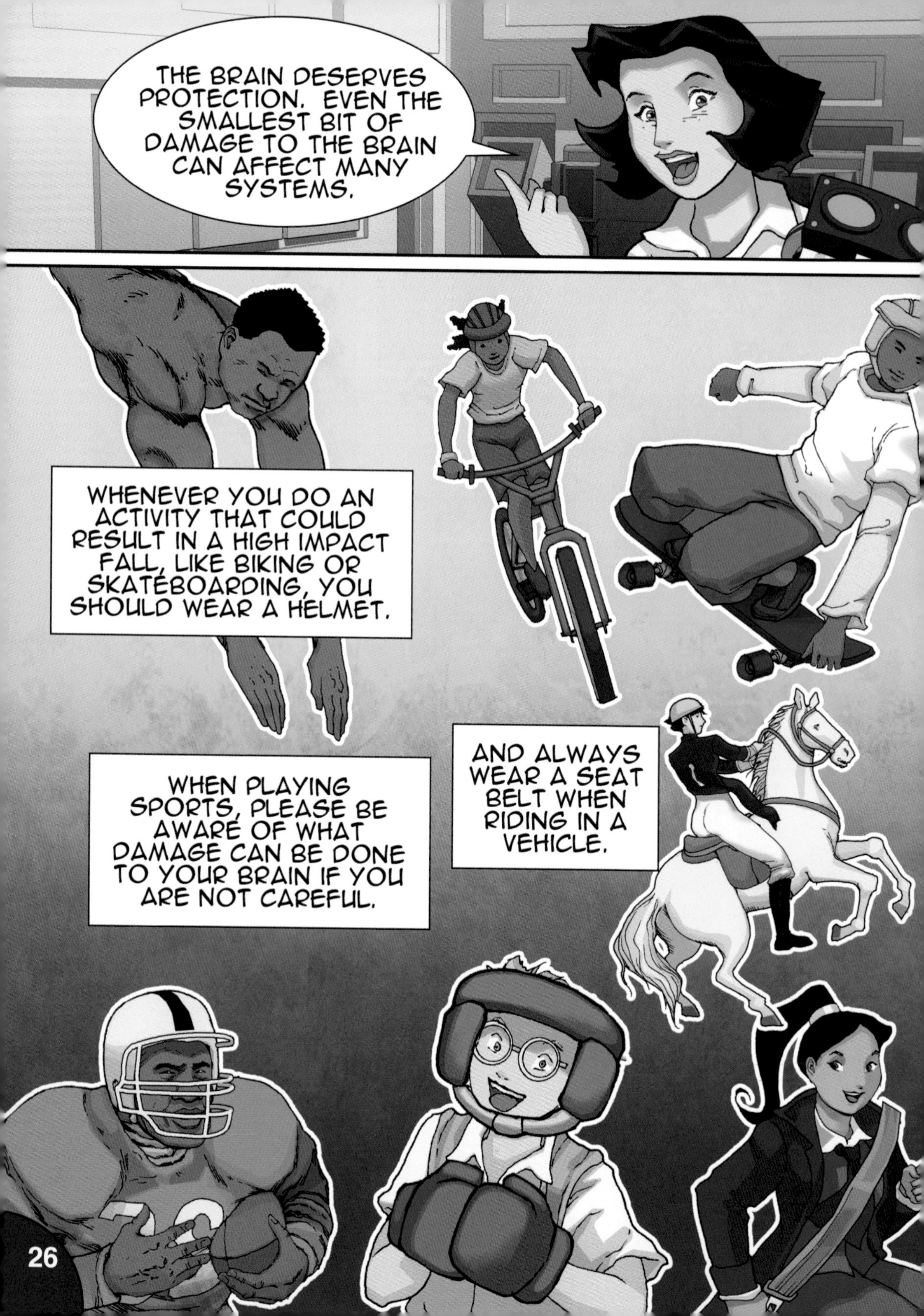

THE BRAIN DESERVES PROTECTION. EVEN THE SMALLEST BIT OF DAMAGE TO THE BRAIN CAN AFFECT MANY SYSTEMS.
WHENEVER YOU DO AN ACTIVITY THAT COULD RESULT IN A HIGH IMPACT FALL, LIKE BIKING OR SKATEBOARDING, YOU SHOULD WEAR A HELMET.
WHEN PLAYING SPORTS, PLEASE BE AWARE OF WHAT DAMAGE CAN BE DONE TO YOUR BRAIN IF YOU ARE NOT CAREFUL.
AND ALWAYS WEAR A SEAT BELT WHEN RIDING IN A VEHICLE.

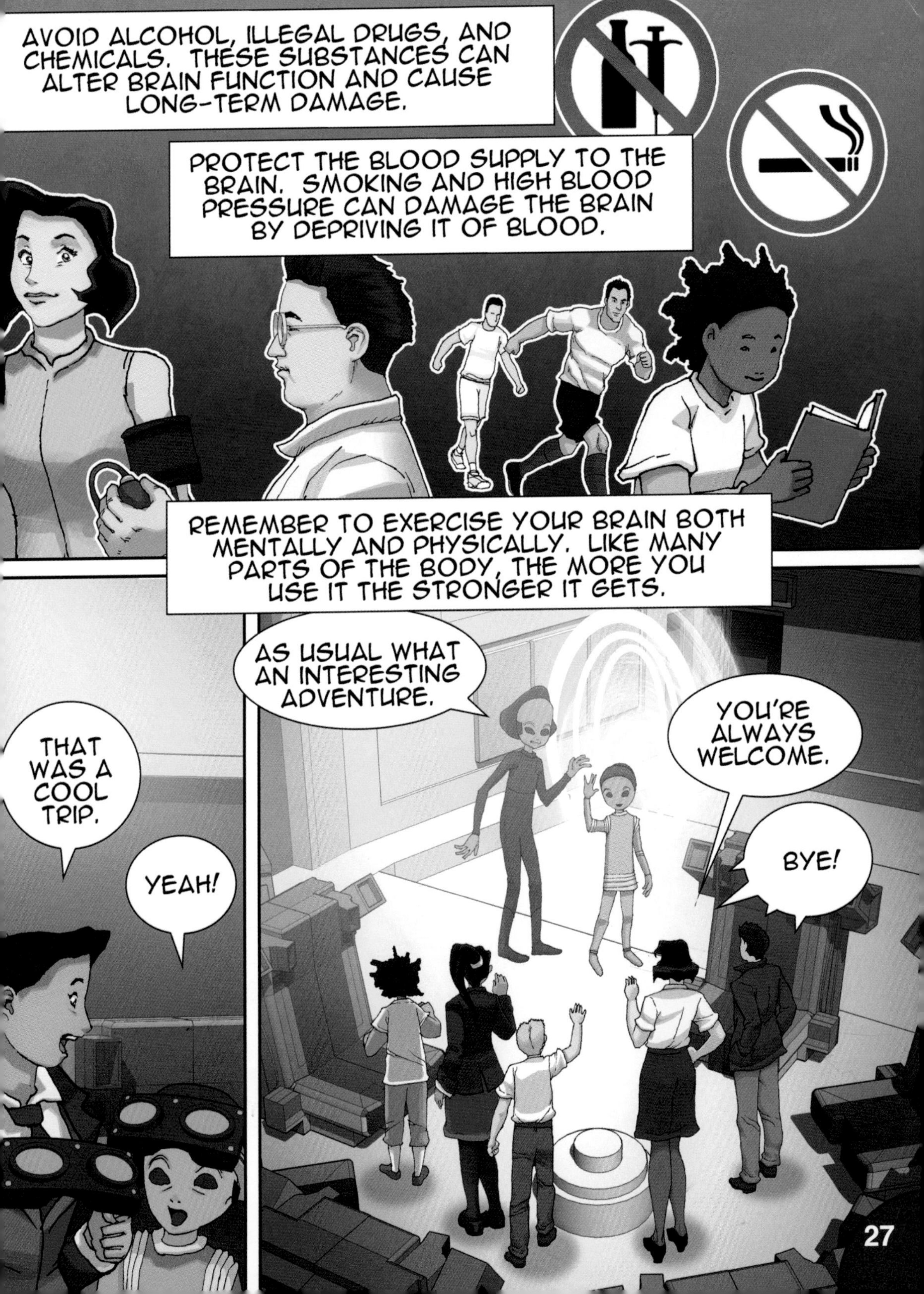
AVOID ALCOHOL, ILLEGAL DRUGS, AND CHEMICALS. THESE SUBSTANCES CAN ALTER BRAIN FUNCTION AND CAUSE LONG-TERM DAMAGE.
PROTECT THE BLOOD SUPPLY TO THE BRAIN. SMOKING AND HIGH BLOOD PRESSURE CAN DAMAGE THE BRAIN BY DEPRIVING IT OF BLOOD.
REMEMBER TO EXERCISE YOUR BRAIN BOTH MENTALLY AND PHYSICALLY. LIKE MANY PARTS OF THE BODY, THE MORE YOU USE IT THE STRONGER IT GETS.
THAT WAS A COOL TRIP.
YEAH!
AS USUAL WHAT AN INTERESTING ADVENTURE.
YOU'RE ALWAYS WELCOME.
BYE!

The Brain: A Diagram

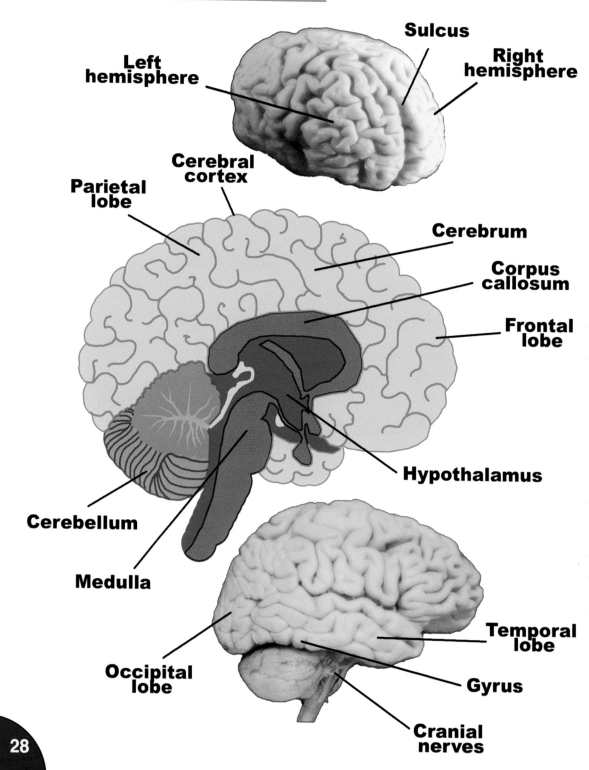

Sulcus

Left hemisphere

Right hemisphere

Cerebral cortex

Parietal lobe

Cerebrum

Corpus callosum

Frontal lobe

Hypothalamus

Cerebellum

Medulla

Occipital lobe

Temporal lobe

Gyrus

Cranial nerves

Fun Facts

There are three membranes called meninges
otecting your brain. The first membrane, the pia mater,
nnects to the brain. On top of that is the arachnoid. The
er closest to the skull is the dura mater.

Have you ever had a headache that hurt so bad it felt
e your brain was throbbing? That's because it was!
migraine headache begins when blood vessels in the
ain narrow. This lets less blood and oxygen into the
ain, which makes the brain ask for more. When the
ain sends the message that it needs more blood and
ygen, other blood vessels expand. Then they throb,
using a pounding pain.

Neurons are the oldest and longest cells in the body!
ople have many of the same neurons for their whole
.

Glossary

abstract – relating to something that doesn't represent a real object but expresses ideas or emotions.

cavity – an unfilled space within the body.

component – a part of something; an ingredient.

impact – to strike with force.

nervous system – the system that transports impulses within the body. The brain, nerves, and spinal cord are all parts of the nervous system.

perception – awareness of the elements around one.

synapse – the point where nerve impulses pass from one to another.

Web Sites

To learn more about the brain, visit ABDO Group online at **www.abdopublishing.com**. Web sites about the brain are featured on our Book Links page. These links are routinely monitored and updated to provide the most current information available.

About the Author

Joeming Dunn is both a general practice physician and the owner of one of the largest comic companies in Texas, Antarctic Press. A graduate of Austin College in Sherman and the University of Texas Medical Branch in Galveston, Dunn has currently settled in San Antonio.

Dr. Dunn has written or co-authored texts in both the medical and graphic novel fields. He met his wife, Teresa, in college, and they have two bright and lovely girls, Ashley and Camerin. Ashley has even helped some with his research for these Magic Wagon books.

About the Illustrator

Rod Espinosa is a graphic novel creator, writer, and illustrator. Espinosa was born in the Philippines in Manila. He graduated from the Don Bosco Technical College and the University of Santo Tomas.

Espinosa has worked in advertising, software entertainment, and film. Today, he lives in San Antonio, Texas, and produces stunning graphic novels including *Dinowars, Neotopia, Metadocs, Battle Girlz, Alice in Wonderland, Stop TB!,* and *Prince of Heroes*. His graphic novel *Courageous Princess* was nominated for an Eisner Award.

Index